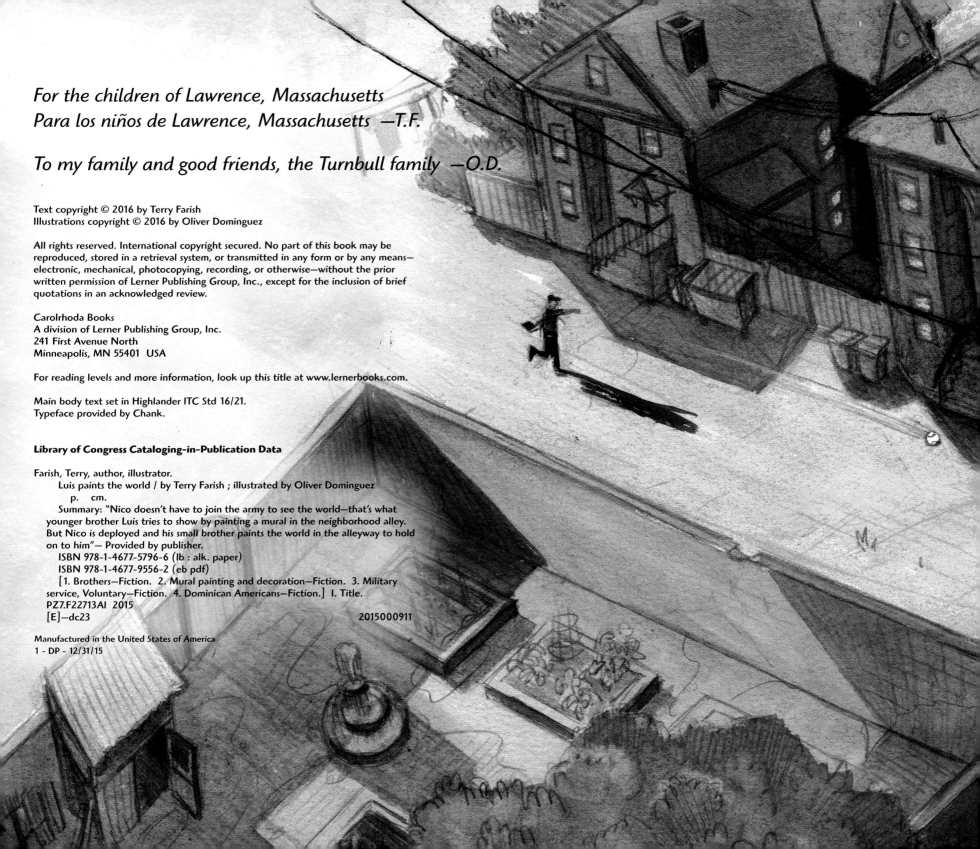

For the children of Lawrence, Massachusetts
Para los niños de Lawrence, Massachusetts —T.F.

To my family and good friends, the Turnbull family —O.D.

Text copyright © 2016 by Terry Farish
Illustrations copyright © 2016 by Oliver Dominguez

Carolrhoda Books
A division of Lerner Publishing Group, Inc.
241 First Avenue North
Minneapolis, MN 55401 USA

For reading levels and more information, look up this title at www.lernerbooks.com.

Main body text set in Highlander ITC Std 16/21.
Typeface provided by Chank.

Library of Congress Cataloging-in-Publication Data

Farish, Terry, author, illustrator.
    Luis paints the world / by Terry Farish ; illustrated by Oliver Dominguez
       p.   cm.
    Summary: "Nico doesn't have to join the army to see the world—that's what younger brother Luis tries to show by painting a mural in the neighborhood alley. But Nico is deployed and his small brother paints the world in the alleyway to hold on to him"— Provided by publisher.
    ISBN 978-1-4677-5796-6 (lb : alk. paper)
    ISBN 978-1-4677-9556-2 (eb pdf)
    [1. Brothers—Fiction. 2. Mural painting and decoration—Fiction. 3. Military service, Voluntary—Fiction. 4. Dominican Americans—Fiction.] I. Title.
PZ7.F22713Al 2015
[E]—dc23
                                          2015000911

Manufactured in the United States of America
1 - DP - 12/31/15

Luis Paints the World

Terry Farish

Illustrated by
Oliver Dominguez

CAROLRHODA BOOKS MINNEAPOLIS

Nico winds up.
Luis races and crunches through leaves in the alleyway. He is ready. The ball sails. Luis catches it—*smack*—in his oversized glove.

"Will you be back before it snows?" Luis calls. "And we can play at the Parque de las Ardillas?"

"No, man, I'll be gone. Seeing the world. Just like the army promised."

"Can I go too?" Luis says. "To see the world?"

But Nico is hauling open his squeaky car door, heading out to see his buddies. "Not leaving till morning," he calls to Luis. "Catch ya before I go."

Inside, Nico's duffel waits by the door.

Nico's car rattles away.

Luis tries to slide inside the duffel.

Mami discovers Luis's legs and hauls him out.

"You're not going to the army too," she says.

"Where is the army?" Luis asks.

"Far away."

Mami returns to stirring sugar in the skillet for the flan.

Nico loves flan. Who will cook him flan far away?

"Naranja dulce," Mami sings, *"limón partido."* Sweet honey orange, a slice of lemon.

Luis says, "Mami, why are you singing about oranges and lemons?"

"Oranges are sweet," she says. "Like you kids. But Nico, *aiii.* Good-byes are sour like lemons."

The moon rises.

Luis puts on his brother's giant
boots. Outside, the lopsided
moon lights the alleyway.
He listens for the squeal of
Nico's engine. Any minute.

Can't his brother see
the world from here?

Mami shakes out the rug at the back door.
She sings, "*Naranja dulce, limón partido . . .*"

Luis brings his paint and brush from the shed.
He paints an orange orange on the alleyway
wall. Then another and another.

He thinks, "What if Nico goes far away and he doesn't come back?" Luis's belly swoops.

He paints a million yellow lemons.

Then the paint wants to swoop. He swoops the brush around to the left. He swoops it around to the right.

Luis paints his house on the wall.

He paints the river. It loops outside his bedroom window to the Parque de las Ardillas, where they play baseball, and to the bodega with trays of *pan de agua*.

He paints two boys—one tall, tall as David Ortiz, one short as a bat.

He paints the world.

Headlights light the wall.

"What's this?" Nico calls.

Luis's grin is sweet and as wide as the moon. "It's the world. So now you don't have to go."

Nico kneels by Luis. He wipes a glop of paint from Luis's cheek.

Luis takes Nico's camouflage jacket. Puts it on. Then he runs.

Inside, Mami takes the flan from the oven.

Luis tries to spoon the flan slowly into his mouth, because when he's done he has to go to bed. It tastes sweet and smooth and disappears too quickly on his tongue.

Nico gives Mami a blue phone that sparkles.

He gives Luis his old mitt and a thick new paintbrush.

They chase and they holler, till Nico lands Luis in his bed.

Fear swoops in. Luis holds tight to Nico.

"Bye, kid." Nico slips his grip.

Luis watches him till the door clicks shut. He squeezes the mitt. He squeezes the paintbrush. Then he squeezes his eyes shut.

In the morning, the duffel is gone.

Luis sits where Nico's car used to be.

The next day, he pulls out
more paint. He swoops it
on the wall. He makes the
river longer. It snakes up the
alleyway past the next house.

Every night Luis and Mami send a text to Nico.

"KLK." *Qué lo que?* What's happening?

Mami sends a picture of Luis by the wall.

Nico sends back a picture of a boy. "Kid I saw here," he writes. The boy is walking with a bicycle. Beyond are jagged mountain peaks.

Down the river, Luis paints the boy and the bicycle.

Now they are in the world.

Ciel from next door watches, her mouth in an O.

The air chills. Icicles glitter over the river rushing down the alleyway wall.

Luis tries to paint. It won't stick on the frozen concrete. But he loves the goopy paint and tries a little on the kitchen wall till Mami says, "No!"

Nico sends a picture of a turquoise cart in a market. It holds bananas stacked high.

When the snow melts, Luis adds a cart and bananas to the alleyway world.

The sun warms the ground. Summer smells like honeysuckle.

Luis and Mami bend their heads over the phone. They have checked all week. No picture.

Luis asks, "How long before Nico comes home?"

"Muy pronto," Mami says. "Pero, Luis, sometimes people, they move on. They don't come back for the baseball. Even the flan."

"Yes, they do," Luis whispers.

Luis's shoes pinch his toes. *Ouch.*

School is starting again.

Nico texts, "Good luck, kid."

Luis paints his brother in a
Red Sox baseball cap and a jersey
with the number 34.

"Promise me," he says to his picture.
"You'll come home. And stay."

Mami calls from the stoop, "No
más. Enough. Okay?"

"Un minuto más?" Luis calls.

Mami lifts her arms to the moon.

It is fall again.

Ciel comes with her own brush.
"Purple!" she says.

Luis nods. She paints violet streaks
on the mountains.

Mami comes out to the
alleyway. Luis hands her
a brush.

She takes in the world
while she thinks.

Mami paints a *panadería* on the banks of the river.
Steam swirls—the bread is hot from the oven.

More neighbors come with brushes.

The alleyway blooms.

Still, Luis can't forget what Mami said, that some people don't come back for the baseball or the flan.

But some people do.

One day, when the leaves start to crinkle . . .

Luis sees his brother, walking up the alleyway.

He puts down his paintbrush.

He wants to be mad and say,
"You have to promise."

But Nico is on his knees.

Luis rushes toward his brother.

And the alleyway wall swoops and
flows, the world rich with color.

Author's Note

Luis and Nico's story takes place in Lawrence, Massachusetts, a city rich in culture and in art reflecting its communities.

The city was built on the Merrimack River, where waterfalls generated power for textile mills. From early on, Lawrence was called Immigrant City as people from Ireland, Poland, Lebanon, Germany, Italy, Canada, and other countries came to work in the mills. Today about three-fourths of Lawrence families are Latino or Hispanic, many from the Dominican Republic and Puerto Rico. Mural artists have depicted the city's history and cultures on tall buildings and in neighborhoods.

I worked as the children's librarian at the Lawrence Public Library for several years, beginning in 2003, and one year I followed the work of young artists from the Greater Lawrence Educational Collaborative Alternative High School. They worked with the Essex Art Center's SPROUT (Splattered Paint Revealed on Ur Turf) program and Lawrence CommunityWorks to design a mural for peace. They painted the mural in an alleyway in the city's North Common neighborhood. It was the work of these students, who painted bright stars and a light hand and a dark hand surrounding Earth, that inspired *Luis Paints the World*.

Glossary

flan: a rich and creamy custard-like treat, made with eggs and sweetened condensed milk. The sugar Mami stirs in the skillet becomes caramelized and makes a sweet crust at the bottom of the flan.

"Naranja Dulce (Sweet Orange)": an old folk song about saying good-bye that traveled from Spain to Mexico and the Caribbean islands of the Dominican Republic and Puerto Rico. Children in many cities in the United States learn and sing the song at home and in their communities.

> *Naranja dulce, limón partido. Dame un abrazo, que yo te pido.*
> Sweet honey orange, a slice of lemon, dear. Give me a hug, keep me in your heart.

pan de agua: "water bread," Dominican bread or breakfast rolls made from flour, yeast, water, and a pinch of salt. The bread is golden crispy on the outside with a soft center.

Parque de las Ardillas: "Squirrel Park," a name give by many Dominican children to the large park in downtown Lawrence. It is also called Campagnone Common.